The Clint Faraday Mysteries
#10
... Or So the Gods Said

Clint is having a discussion on the bus with a priest from The Church of Absolute Truth in Life .. or something such. The conversation gets weird. There are always a few nutcases here, so he doesn't think much of it – until the murders.

Clint Faraday
#10
...Or So the Gods Said

Contents

About the author

CD was born in Lakeland, Florida. His education is in genetics and botany. He has traveled over much of the world, particularly when he was in music as a rock rhythm guitarist with some well-known bands in the late sixties and early seventies. He has worked as a high steel worker and as a longshoreman, clerk, orchidist, bar owner, salvage yard manager and landscaper – among other things.

CD began writing fiction in 1984 and has more than 115 books published as of this time in SciFi, murder, orchid culture and various other fields. He now resides in Bocas del Toro and David, Panamá, where he continues research into epiphytic plants. He loves the culture of the indigenous people and counts a majority of his closer friends among that group. Several have "adopted" him as their father. He funds those he can afford through the universities where they have all excelled. "The Indios are very intelligent people, they are simply too poor (in material things and money. Culturally, they are very wealthy) to pursue higher education."

CD loves Panamá and the people. He plans to spend the rest of his life in the paradise that is Panamá
- Estrelita Suarez V.

CD is involved in research of natural cancer cure at this time. It has proven effective in all cases, so far. It is based on a plant that has been in use for thousands of years, is safe, available, and cheap. He has studied botany, and was cured of a serious lymphoma with use of the plant, *Ambrosia peruviana.*

Information about this cure is free on the FaceBook page, Ambrosia peruviana for cancer. CD asks only that all who try it please report on its effectiveness on that group.

Clint groaned inwardly when he got on the bus to Chiriqui Grande from David. The only seat open was next to a thin tight-lipped sour-looking man in his early thirties who had a Bible in his hands – which was probably why no one sat next to him. Clint nodded shortly, said "Buenos," shoved his small maleta under the seat and sat.

"Good morning, Brother," the man announced. "I am The Most Reverend Emanuel Howland Charleston. May God bless our journey through these savage dangerous pagan lands with his never-ending mercy."

"Whatever," Clint replied. "Faraday. One of the savage pagans."

The man looked a little embarrassed. "I meant no disparagement. These misguided people are unaware of their damnation for the unmoral lives they lead. I am here to attempt to educate them in The Way."

"Oh, really? `Savage dangerous pagans' isn't disparagement of them?" Clint asked innocently. "Perhaps we have a different dictionary. I find most of these people to be very moral and peaceful people.

"I'm not interested in your brand of religion. Religion's a personal matter. I would never try to force my beliefs – or my lack of them – on anyone else. That's never appreciated."

"I fear for their eternal souls! The Bible tells us plainly what is the fate of those who will not accept the gracious offer of The Lord for eternal peace and plenty!"

"Uh-huh. And five hundred other cults also have the ultimate answer that excludes anyone who doesn't follow their idiot codes."

"Sir! I resent that! I have found the ultimate truth, and it is demonstrated daily for all but the deliberately blind to see and hear! There is but one path, one very clearly marked, to truth and salvation! The Bible tells us exactly which path leads to heaven and which leads to hell!"

"Oh? You didn't read the part about spouting your religion on the streets being a fast way to guarantee you the hell you're so afraid of? I believe the part I mean is something like `... for they shall not know the kingdom of heaven,' or something in that vein," Clint asked a bit stiffly. "Maybe you should check your concordance for the reference. It would seem to me you've taken a dangerous detour from your path to salvation.

"We should maybe discuss other things. I don't prance around the fact I don't like to argue religion in public."

"But you do believe in an all-powerful god, surely!"

"Ask yourself, `If there is an all-powerful god, why am I needed?' All such a god would have to do is put the socalled facts in the minds of everyone at birth. The least thing would be to make the announcement where there would be no question."

"But every sunrise and sunset demonstrates the undisputable answer! Every flower and tree shouts the truth to us!"

"Really. Ever smelled *Bulbphyllum putridum*? Beautiful flower. A small whiff of the odor and you vomit. How about cockroaches and scorpions? What evidence of god is there? A red sky in morning is an old warning that storms are to the east and will come toward you. The sunrise and sunset make statements, I guess, but they can be downright ominous warnings. It's the nature of light, not a picture painted by god."

"But those are not things of god, necessarily. Satan has placed such things to deter us in our thoughts and divert us from the true path!"

"So now Satan can create? I thought only God could create. Isn't that what your Bible tells you?"

"You, sir, are among the damned! You will not see the truth when it is demonstrated by the very fact you exist!

"I am not descrying your sad life. Honestly, I am most concerned for your immortal soul!"

"I said, from the first, I don't swallow your brand of crap. I'll appreciate it if you save it for someone who gives a damn about it. It bores me and begins to get on my nerves. As the natives say, No moleste!"

"But, sir! I'm in great fear for your personal damnation if you refuse to see the True Path!"

"Here's a quarter for your concern. Use it to spread the words or something. Just don't try to spread it to me, Okay?"

Clint noticed how he seemed to be totally insulted – but he took the quarter. Clint almost laughed out loud at him. The man in the seat behind let out a little snort. Clint looked at him and grinned, which got him a big grin in return. The man had intensely blue eyes, rare in the Panamanian people. Clint thought they must be contacts. Panamanians did like blue eyes.

About an hour later, as they were crossing the Enel Fortuna dam, The Most Reverend Whatever put his head against the seat in front of them and was mumbling a prayer in what approached abject terror. He was reacting to the magnificent vista outside by never glancing out, but the dam is not something you can ignore. The view to one side was of a beautiful river/reservoir and a drop on the other of several hundred meters to the picturesque river, which seemed a small creek, from the distance. Clint felt an urge to throw the ass's words back at him, so pointed to the valley to their left, then to the river, and said such magnificence did make one feel a reverence. It was humbling. Such a pity man built that dam in that spot, forming the reservoir, not god.

He got a very sickly nod from his seat partner. "I'm afraid of heights. Since birth."

Clint forbore saying that must be a punishment from god for something his parents must have done. It couldn't be a punishment to a newborn baby, surely!

He could picture the reply. It was a test of faith. Clint would point out that a newborn baby needed a test, by an all-knowing god, of faith? Why would any test of any type be needed by this all-knowing, all-powerful god?

It might pass the time, but was hopeless. No one could reach the type.

On the other side of the dam, Emanuel said he often wondered what God's plan was for him that would include such a burden. He only knew for certain that God had a plan for him, and that it wasn't for him to know or understand what that plan may be.

Again, Clint was tempted to ask what the purpose of acute acrophobia in a disciple could possibly be. Wouldn't that tend to deter him from spreading the word in these mountainous places?

Yeah, right! The answer would be that he went to such places in spite of the phobia to serve God! *That* could be what the test was about! There was a paradoxical answer to anything. Hopeless.

Just before Mali, Emanuel said he suspected that there was more than one god. There was one for Earth, but each world where there were men might have a different one.

Clint said the Bible stated there was only one god.

"One God for this world! That is my question. I pray daily for an answer. I have studied religion as history. I have to agree that there were possibly or even probably other gods in ancient times. God was victorious in expunging them from this world. I believe this happened in the earliest times of the Greek civilization. The later Greeks and the Romans simply took the older religion – the older gods – and continued them. There were, and still are, followers of those old religions.

"I also have some questions as to the writing of the New Testament. I see some very frightening possibilities. It bothers me that it was written so long after Christ's ascendance into heaven. The writers, if they were who is claimed, would necessarily be more than a hundred years old, and people didn't live nearly that long back then.

"I base my philosophy on the old testament and try to discern which parts of the New Testament are real and which are added later."

"That's the Jewish faith," Clint answered.

"Perhaps. Much of it is, but interpretations vary, even among the Jews. The Koran is also much like the Old Testament. The problem I have is that God was almost viciously cruel and was a greatly-feared being. I find that is not what ... I don't know! I believe in a loving and merciful God, not a vengeful God!"

Clint said he would be better accepted if he would simply lay his questions out to people and ask for help finding answers. Don't try to impress a faith on people who'll later learn exactly how deep his own questions are of that faith.

"You have found the deep basis for my dilemma, I fear. My faith was always very strong, from a very young age. My parents were, believe it or not, agnostics bordering on atheists. Hippies. A man of very deep faith took me in when I ran away from that sordid drug-induced lifestyle and introduced me to The Faith. He was not so driven to ... spread the word, as it were. He merely had me read the Bible to find strength to cross the dangerous path into the future, for a map of which path leads to the light, and which to the darkness.

"My first fears were from the Old Testament. The vengeful, cruel concept of God. I found great solace in the New Testament – but was plagued with doubts and questions.

"I decided the truth was there, so pursued that truth with intense study. I was twenty eight when I knew I had the ultimate answer, so then set out to help my fellow man navigate the path. I never wavered a millimeter from that path. There was never a time when anything whatever clouded my vision. I spent more than two years in that quest and found that the US is deeply decadent. It is frighteningly so. Everything is the money, the economy, the banks ... pointless pursuits that have become so ingrained in the daily lives of most that they are unaware of how they are controlled by a few powerful people.

"I am not a conspiracy believer, yet it is obvious there is some kind of control of all of our lives. It is just that I cannot find a way to have even a minor influence against this travesty. None is so blind, and all that.

"I decided to travel to places where I may make a difference in the lives of people. I do care. Deeply.

"I find they have given me questions that make no sense whatever in their answers. I find the native indigenous people to be very simple and very unbelieving, yet they are also well-suited to the very free life here. I wonder that I do more damage than good with my beliefs. I also find observing them and their ways leaves me with great doubts about what I perceive to be ultimate truth. It is horrible!

"You are a very accepting person, I feel. I am aware that you find me ... irritating. Possibly obnoxious. Perhaps there is reason. I watched the way the indigenous people greeted you as you entered the bus. You are one of them, in spirit, which was the philosophy of my parents which I rejected.

"I have no warmth in my life. You have it everywhere. You can see how troubled my soul is about this. Nothing is as I first perceived ... that is not the word. I expected it to be."

"It's all about individual perceptions," Clint replied, quoting his weird musician/botanist friend, Dave. "Reality is situational. Truth is situational. It's a matter of what you might call the angle from which you observe it. Life here is both very hard and very easy. The Indios don't need the same things people in cities and socalled civilized areas need.

"I'm not talking about 'things'. I'm talking about the psychological points."

"I understand that they have no word for 'Thank you' in their language, yet they quite obviously appreciate help, in many areas."

"They touch to say 'Thank you.' Words aren't necessary. They have a beautiful lifestyle. They live in paradise, and belong here. We don't. I don't believe in gods, but I say 'Thank you' every day to whatever force may be that I'm accepted by them. I love the Indios. They don't need lessons in a belief or faith or whatever. That's an unwarranted incursion into their lives.

"If you want a suggestion, simply observe them and try to understand where they're coming from. Almost everything they don't seem to have turns out to be a thing they don't need and are better off without."

He nodded. "I feel that is probably my course. I must question my life and wonder if my mission is a negative thing."

"It's neutral. You can't affect these people. Stop questioning your own, as you call it, course in life. Simply wait and observe. Maybe the answers are too obvious to see from inside the box. Get *out* of the box for awhile.

"You don't have to change the way you live, or whatever. Just step back and take a good long solid look at what the real world is. It just might surprise you as to how the way you've always looked at things from inside the states or inside your psychological box is almost the reverse of reality.

"Reality can be viciously mean – or delightful. You won't know if you don't go there."

"I believe you. I've been a blind ... maybe just an ignorant soul who looked for answers to the wrong questions in the wrong places at the wrong time. I'm really, as you would say, screwed up, I suspect."

"Give it time and distance. Lay back and relax. Meet people without expectations. That's the Indio philosophy. It boils down to the fact we're all individuals. The same things aren't needed or wanted by everyone."

He nodded again and sat back to look thoughtful. The bus was going across a bridge where there was a washout during the bad weather three years ago. There was a drop of over two hundred meters, right outside the window. Emanuel looked down at it and giggled.

"That didn't bother me at all! It was exciting and beautiful!"

"Maybe the fall you were so afraid of isn't a physical one."

"I think perhaps you are right." He reached to touch Clint's hand. It was obviously the way the Indios said "Thank you" that Clint had explained to him.

"As the gods said, 'The truth shall make you free!' I think maybe that's the one truth in all this mess."

"That's a fallacy, in a lot of ways. Don't fall into another philosophical trap. Another view of the truth can enslave you as much as the old one."

He touched Clint's hand again.

Clint walked along the dock to greet Moises and Andres, two close Indio friends. He asked about the comarca and they swapped a few stories over coffee. Things were, as always, just moving along in the way of things. Clint told about the overly-religious passenger on the bus. He said there was a very small chance he was able to make the man step back and look at reality instead of some place and code that existed only in his mind.

"I imagine that, in the estados, you could never reach his mind," Andres, the more philosophical of the two, said. "Here? Who knows?

"The predictions you so studiously avoided indicated a period of tranquility for the people on the comarca. It has, once again, proven correct – so far."

They discussed the predictions in the sunset that led Clint to a strange case (*Omen*) and other things. It was a pleasant time. Clint stayed at a friend's place in Chiriqui Grande, then took his boat to Bocas Town in the morning to check on things.

Things were the same as he left them in Bocas Town. Clint spent some time at his neighbor, Judi Lum's place, catching up on the gossip. He told about his friends in Chiriqui Grande and about things being, as usual, tranquil and pleasant on the comarca. He told about his trip to Las Tablas and Chitre, and about the preacher on the bus.

"I hate it when somebody tries to make me accept some nutcase religion. I hope you did make him question what he believed enough that he'll stop doing it.

"Yeah! Get real! They never do."

They decided to go to the Lemon Grass for Thai food that evening, then Clint went back home to straighten out his files and answer what of his e-mails he intended to answer. He had more than fifty waiting. If he actually won all the scam lotteries and bank transfers and such on them he would have over ten billion dollars in the bank. As Judi so recently said, "Yeah! Get real!"

There were eight legitimate mails he answered. None of them critical.

He went into town to talk with people, then laid around for a couple of hours until time to pick Judi up for the dinner. They had a good time and ate an exceptional meal. They went out of town a little way to a bar where the Indios spent a lot of time. They stayed, talking with a number of them (Judi was learning the dialect), then called it a night when the "drunk hours" approached.

The Indios have no resistance to alcohol. If a majority of them have one beer they won't stop until they're either drunk or broke. They will most generally change to seco or other rum after a couple of beers.

They evolved without alcohol. The Europeans and Asians evolved with it. Gringos had built-in resistance, many of them, and could take a drink or three, then go home. What always amazed Clint was how the Indios could get so drunk they literally passed out in a ditch, then they'd get up in the morning and go to work. If he got half that drunk he'd have a hangover for a week!

Life was strange.

When Clint got home there was a text message on his phone. From Emanuel. He said he was going to go to a few small villages to, as Clint suggested, observe. He promised not to mention religion and to shy away from talking about it if asked.

Where did he get the phone number?

He asked about anyone. Clint was well-known. He sighed and went to bed.

"Clint? This is Moises. I'm still in Chiriqui Grande."

"Coin dega." Clint replied.

"Remember that preacher? Emanuel the Great, or something such? The one on the bus?"

"Uh-huh."

"He stayed here in Chiriqui Grande last night. He didn't say too much about Christ or any of that. He actually made a couple of friends. He seems to really be interested in people. He had to stop himself, it was obvious, a few times from saving souls or whatever.

"Clint, I don't know what's going on. Two men came from Panamá City and were asking about him. We don't like them and they aren't the kind of people we ... we were suspicious, so I told everyone to say they didn't know who they were talking about. When gringos come into our places we mostly act like they're not there. (Not true. The Indios are the most welcoming people in the world!) and deliberately don't remember anything about them. They said they were from the government and that he had problems about his passport. They said they were afraid he was one of those terrorists from the estados.

"I said, if there is anything the indigenos don't give a shit about it is those stupid terrorists or the more stupid people who let them scare them.

"That seemed to anger the one, in some way. I can't imagine why.

"Anyhow, I thought you should know."

"Are the two still there?"

"Yes. They were right here ten minutes ago."

"Thanks, friend. I'll manage to come there to shop or something in a little bit. Maybe I'll accidentally meet them and be able to see what the hell they want – and why."

They chatted a few minutes about everyday things, then Clint hung up and put a few things in his boat. Judi came out on her deck and waved. He called that he was going to Chiriqui Grande. Did she want to go?

She said she'd be ready in five minutes,

He chatted on the way about what was going on in Panamá. He wouldn't mention why he was going to Chiriqui Grande so she wouldn't let it slip that he was there for any specific purpose.

Judi? What? He had slipped a cog? Judi Lum would let something slip?

"What's it about, Clint? You were in Chiriqui Grande yesterday, then suddenly want to go shopping there today?"

He told her. He said the guy was weird enough, but a standard type of weird. He was damned curious as to why anyone would be after him. Particularly with a lame excuse like terrorism in Bocas del Toro, Panamá.

She was the best he'd met at getting information by acting like she wasn't the least interested in whatever.

They came into the dock, where Moises was working on his cayuca. He was adjusting the injectors on his motor.

"Injectors? On a twenty five horsepower outboard?" Judi asked.

"Maybe that's why I can't seem to get it adjusted just right! It doesn't *have* injectors!" he replied.

They joked a bit. Moises said the two were at the hotel,

still asking about Emanuel. He had the word out that it would be a good idea if they had a lot of trouble finding him.

"He took the bus to Changuinola. He wanted to see some of the smaller pueblas to learn the real way of life of the people. I suppose he got off at Rio Uyama or Norteno."

"Point them out to me where they can't see. I'll manage to run into them somewhere," Judi suggested.

"They're hard to miss," Moises replied. "The two big morenos with lots of flashy jewelry. Suits – and you can tell they don't wear suits in whatever they really do. At the hotel."

Judi grinned and said she'd give Clint a ring if she learned anything. She strolled toward the hotel. Clint thought a bit and said to have someone suggest Emanuel went to see Valle de Aguas. There was a tiny chance he got off there, but it was a very unlikely destination.

He went into the town and chatted with a couple of people, then happened to be passing the little restaurant across the street from the hotel when Judi came out with two big blacks. One of them kept trying to paw at her, but she was expert in avoiding that! She saw Clint and waved. Clint waved back and went into the restaurant. She brought the two over and introduced Roberto Smith and his cousin, Willie Silva, from Panamá City, working in immigration for the government looking for a suspected drug smuggler.

"Drug smuggler? I thought ... didn't Jorge say ... terrorist?" Clint asked innocently.

"Oh! Er, we just said that to get information. The truth is, seeing you're a gringo, he was trying to assassinate President Martinelli. We're trying to find him to deport him back to, uh, Canada."

"Isn't it exciting!" Judi cried. "He's the one you were telling me about that sat next to you on the bus and tried to convert you to that silly cult or whatever!"

The two exchanged looks. Willie looked like he just got a fist in the gut.

"That nut? He didn't try to assassinate anybody. He wouldn't have the spine to kill a mouse in the kitchen."

"Er, I guess we'll have to level with you. He absconded with more than a million dollars of the churches money. It was for a fund for construction, now we have a church half built and no money to finish it."

"A million dollars for a church building in a country where there's so much poverty, and where so many need medical and can't afford it?" Judi asked, looking shocked (she was good at that, too). "That's downright sick! It's disgusting!

"So. You sit here wearing two hundred dollar suits and ten thousand dollars worth of jewelry looking for somebody who stole a million dollars for a church building. You ever hear the words `scam' or `corruption?' You're disgusting!"

She got up and walked out.

Moises was out front when she marched out, talking with a gringo tourist who looked a little familiar. Clint was sure he'd seen him somewhere, but couldn't place him. Blond, blue-eyed Swiss or Dane, by the look. Judi grinned at Moises and pointed at Clint. He got the message, and came in to say, "Clint? You asked where that preacher went if we could find out?

"He went to Valle de Aguas, according to Sylvia. He wants to see the Caribbean from the mountains and to see how the people live.

"I see these two mentirosas are with you. They were asking about him, but told three different stories why, so we didn't try to find anything for them. We don't like mentirosas from the government here and we will not cooperate with them in anything."

"Thanks, Moises. They're just government agents. They're alike everywhere in the world. They think they have to make up an exciting lie to get information when it would be faster and easier if they would only bother to tell the truth. Politician and liar are synonyms."

"They're what?"

"They're the same word with different pronunciation."

"Oh. I'm going home. Care to come?"

"I'll be out there next week. Tell everyone I said `oye!' and send my love."

They hugged, then Moises left.

"Maybe I'll go to Valle de Aguas to ... no. Why bother? He's not up to anything. I'll just do my shopping and go back to Bocas.

"Have a nice day or whatever."

They looked embarrassed and grunted. Clint walked out.

Now Clint really was curious. He simply couldn't connect Emanuel with anything to do with crime or terrorism or anything else – other than evangelism. Of course, that could be what made him the perfect agent for some kind of stupid political intrigue.

Moises was waiting near the dock. He said he knew where Emanuel was. Rio Uyama.

Clint went to the dock, where Judi was talking with several of the Indios and their wives and children. She had bought a big bag of cookies to pass out. He told her to take the boat back to Bocas and he'd come later or tomorrow on the bus. He wanted to find out what this was about.

They chatted there for a few minutes with their friends. Judi noticed Willie and Roberto were off to the side, watching them, and told Clint. He got in the boat with her and her packages (while she was there anyhow, she did some shopping) and they headed out toward the islands. When they were out from Punta Robalo she came to the dock and dropped Clint off. He would get a bus there for Rio Uyama.

His celular buzzed. It was Fredrico, with the policia in Chiriqui Grande. He said he heard Clint was in town. It may not mean anything, but Anita Clemento Serena L. died in a strange accident late last night. She was a very powerful and very corrupt woman who had caused several of the gringos in the area a lot of problems to force bribes from them.

"What kind of accident?"

"She had a dangerous electrical fence on her gate. She came home after midnight and got out of her Mercedes automobile to unlock the gate. The disconnect wire on the switch to the lock had rusted through and the wire was off. She touched the gate and it electrocuted her. Fitting, but rather strange.

"You were here yesterday and again today. I wondered

if she was the center of your attention or if it was a coincidence."

"I've heard of her. Nothing good. I didn't have anything concerning her as a reason to be here. I was looking into something very different. From what little I know about her and her family, it was, as you said, fitting.

"It was probably an accident – unless there's something you haven't told me?"

"It is just a small suspicion that I don't have time to investigate now. I can't picture her not having everything, particularly a gate with an electrical connection to more than twenty times the legal limit, in perfect working condition at all times."

"I see. Sad accident. Case closed. If it's some of her crooked friends starting a personal war, maybe they'll kill off a bunch of them."

"We can but hope avidly. If there are anymore incidents I will contact you. Caio!"

"Caio."

Clint wondered. Roberto and Willie? He couldn't picture Emanuel having anything to do with any such thing.

Still?

He walked out to the highway and waited for the bus. He was in the casita when he saw a big car that he'd seen in Chiriqui Grande coming, so managed to be behind the casita when it passed. It was Willie and Roberto. Probably headed for Valle de Aguas.

He got on the bus and off at Rio Uyama. He asked about the preacher at the almacen and was told that he had walked on in toward the village by the river, a ways off the road. Clint saw several people he knew, and stopped to chat. They had all noticed the strange man, but said he didn't say anything about religion to them. He only asked where to find Carlos Rincon, a local landowner. They told him they didn't know much about him because he was never around. What they didn't tell him is that they wouldn't know anything about the crooked ladron if he was around. He was not liked by decent people. Emanuel did say that he had a message for him from some people who mentioned that he had strayed from the true path. That was as close to religion as he came.

Clint went on to the village and found that Emanuel had gone on toward the rancho, about a kilometer toward the west. The very large and ostentatious brick house in the valley. There was another stranger around.

Clint remembered the man in Chiriqui Grande who was talking with Moises.

No. This one was dark and had somewhat longish hair. Panamanian, probably. He was probably just looking around and hadn't spoken with anyone. No one saw his eyes because he was wearing dark glasses.

He met Emanuel about two-thirds of the way there, coming back. He said he talked to a man in Chiriqui Grande who said that Mr. Rincon was someone who could use some counseling about his evil ways and had come to see what it was about, though he suspected that a sharp businessman had gotten the best of his complainer in some deal.

"He is, it seems, in some place near the Pacific. All I wished to do was speak with the man and try to determine the truth. Perhaps I may be of use in such an endeavor. I would not make the faith a part of it except to the extent of showing which passages were pertinent to the problem.

"I find many people who are spoken of as evil are merely

misguided and unable to communicate their true feelings, so hide behind a facade of toughness or such. That is most true in Haiti and Jamaica, and is spreading through many large cities in the states. Miami, Los Angeles, New York, and so forth, where people who are usually very afraid of life pretend a toughness that is not there. It is what they call a macho complex. It is, in greatest part, the direct result of the extreme glorification of violence through the moving pictures and television, with particular attention to this horrible rap music stuff, I fear. The culture is decadent and holds little hope for a good future, anymore. The most negative traits are the ones glorified.

"It always seems to happen. We do what we can to try to help our fellow man to survive with a little self-respect.

"That is the whole thing, you see. No one has self-respect anymore, thus no one respects them. It is a circular trap that few can escape.

"Clint, I fear it is mostly the result of terrible over-population. There is less and less to be spread among more and more people. I believe the people here have found a workable solution. They refuse to fall into the trap of things and greed. The Bible was correct when written, 'Go ye forth and multiply.' That certainly does not hold to the reality of what the world has become. It becomes a basis for one of my concerns as to what is true and what is not in the Bible."

They walked back toward the carretera. Clint listened to him. He still didn't let the possibility Emanuel had killed someone hold any credence.

That meant Roberto and Willie? Were they afraid Emanuel had carried some kind of message to the dead woman, or had learned something from her? Were they looking for him to shut him up?

They were waiting for the bus back to Chiriqui Grande. Clint decided to tell Emanuel about the two. Emanuel honestly seemed totally confused. He thought the idea he was a terrorist or thief was purely and plainly ludicrous. The Bible made it plain that the fate of such was eternal damnation.

He asked Clint if he ever heard of some place called The Tablets, near the Pacific.

"Los Quadernos? No."

"It sounded like that to me. I'll have to find out where they meant. I'm sure – Tables, maybe?"

"Las Tablas?"

"Yes, I think so."

"It's near Chitre, on the Pacific. That's where Rincon is?"

"Well, the girl said he often stayed at his place there. She never knew exactly where he would be at any given time. He moves around constantly. It's probably a waste of time to go where he may or may not be. I'll just have to find another project I suppose."

The bus to David came, and he boarded. Clint waited for the one to Changuinola and headed home.

"Hi, Clint! Learn anything?" Judi called.

"Nothing new. I think they think he knows something and want to shut him up."

She waved and went inside. Clint went inside his own place and called Fredrico to ask if anything new had come up. Nothing of any real importance.

"Any word of anything strange in Rio Uyama or Valle de Aguas?"

"Strange? Not for the area. A fight that two people cut each up a little, but not too serious. A girl died of snakebite in Rio Uyama. Back on a ranch, away from the village. No medical close."

"The Rincon ranch?" Clint asked, perking up.

"No. Castillo ranch."

Clint chatted a minute, then hung up. If it had been Rincon's place he would have had a very bad feeling about things.

He went into Bocas Town and met a girl from Copenhagen who wanted a little fun on her vacation, but couldn't communicate with the locals very well. She spent the night with him, no promises or strings. It was a great night.

When Clint was up and about in the morning he made a few calls to find out what he could about the girl who died of snakebite. For some reason, it wouldn't get off his mind.

Not much. She was a local girl who had a bit of a reputation as a part-time prostitute and a petty thief. She worked at times for all the big landowners. They had ways to keep her in check, she knew it, so she didn't take things from them.

Clint couldn't see any reason anyone would want her dead. It was probably just a snakebite.

He thought a bit about it and called Frederico to ask what he knew about Rincon. Other than that he wasn't popular, not much.

"He has a place in Las Tablas?"

"I can find out. I'll have them call you and you can ask what you like."

Half an hour later a man called from Las Tablas and said

that Rincon had a large place out near the ocean. He wasn't popular there, and stayed to himself. Clint thanked him and went into town, where he ran into Willie and Roberto. They said they had traced Emanuel to Bocas Town, they thought, but he wasn't there.

"Oh, I saw him on his way back to Chiriqui Grande or on to David. He thinks this area is too primitive for his tastes or something."

"When?!"

"Late yesterday. I was visiting some friends in Miramar, and he came by to wait on the bus at the casita there."

They seemed anxious to leave so Clint waved and went on to chat with a few friends in various places. Willie and Roberto almost ran to the water taxi to Almirante. It seemed they had a sudden need to go to David. Strange.

About eleven Clint got a call. It was Roberto. He said he was in David, and that Emanuel had caught a bus for Santiago. Did Clint have any idea where he was headed?

"Probably going to stay in Santiago a day and head back to Panamá City. The country scene wasn't much to his liking."

Roberto hung up suddenly. Clint smirked. He could picture the wild drive to Santiago this time of night.

Would they be able to find if he went to Las Tablas? *Did* he go to Las Tablas?

Clint forgot it and went home.

"Mr. Faraday? I am Evelina Donatti, a friend of a friend. I was asked to call you by some strange preacher or something.

"I'm in Las Tablas. He says you will know who he is and I am to tell you 'They're here. What is happening?' He is afraid they are thugs. That is all."

Clint sighed. How did he get caught up in this kind of thing? What was he supposed to do about it?

"Thanks," he replied. She rung off.

Screw it. Clint and Ben went fishing. When he got back home he had another voice mail. Julio Estevez, a close friend in the national police serving a term in Chitre said to please call him.

Clint called. It seemed they had a body, a man named Rincon. Clint had asked about him?

"Just curious about some of the things I heard. It seems he wasn't much liked anywhere around here. What happened?"

"We aren't sure. He seems to have been hit by a car and was found laying on the road. It is suspicious because he was not the kind ever to be walking along the road there. He drove his fancy car everywhere he went."

"Maybe he just had car trouble," Clint said. "Where's his car?"

"We will, of course, determine that. Perhaps that is what happened."

Clint hung up. He was really curious now.

What the hell? He hadn't seen much of Las Tablas. It was supposed to be a great area. He'd go. He called Judi and said he was going to Chitre and Las Tablas. Want to come along?

She wanted to, but had some projects she couldn't put on hold right now.

He packed a few things – he always traveled light – and headed for Changuinola. He'd rather take the bus, but this was too far. He got a flight to Santiago with a change at David airport from Changuinola. He managed to get there at a little after four, so took a bus to Chitre. It was a little after 9:30 when he reached Chitre, so he stayed the night there and went to Las Tablas on the early bus. It didn't take long to find Willie and Roberto. They were at the hotel restaurant, trying to find where Emanuel had gone. They spotted him when he walked in and demanded to know why he was there.

"Go fuck yourselves!" he said easily. "I don't answer to you for where I go anywhere or why. Get out of my face!"

"I'm sorry!" Willie cried. "We went about that the wrong way. We're so used to no one ever answering questions ... we're half crazy! We can't let that character get away!"

"Try a little tranquilidad. Just say hello and what are you here for? The fiesta? You'll get answers. Make demands and people react to you the way they've always seen you. Two big bad government assholes."

"Can we talk?" Roberto asked. "This is getting out of hand, all the way around."

Clint shrugged and went to their table to order huevos revueltos and hojaldres with lots of coffee.

"We're not government," Willie finally said.

"That was obvious from the first time I saw you. I just waited to see if you'd tell me what's going on and why you're after some religious nutcase."

"We say we're government so people will give us infor-mation." Roberto said. "They see though us from the get-go. Why? How?"

"You don't dress like government. That's the states where anybody in the government can wear two hundred dollar suits and expensive jewelry. Your shoes cost what a government official here makes in about a month and a half.

"What are you? CIA, with a lot of stupid TV training? Watch how Hollywood portrays you and think anybody anywhere is idiot enough to swallow that crap?

"To these people, that crap is more a comedy show than any picture of reality.

"Come on! An armored truck goes up a ramp and hits a helicopter, then there's an explosion that makes Bikini look like a firecracker?"

"We're not CIA. We do some work with them. We actually work with Interpol," Willie replied. "I agree about the movies. Unbelievable crap!"

"You know I have sources where I can verify that in about ten seconds?"

"No! We work *with* Interpol, not *for* them," Roberto protested. "Willie takes the government man act too far. It won't fly with you."

"So? What's the crap about Emanuel the Holy or what-ever?"

"We've been trying to figure that out," Roberto answered. "It seems that everywhere he goes people end up dead. They're usually the worst kind of garbage, it's true. No loss – but we want to know how he does it and gets away with it so easily. The Interpol thing is because too many of the ones who end up dead are collectors of art and so forth who have a number of items that are, shall we say, not very well certified as to their source. Too often, they're stuff stolen in Europe.

"Did you know Rincon was under suspicion of having a Rembrandt that disappeared from a Stropshire collection fifteen years ago? I'd bet a bundle that we'll find it when we search his house. He also had a Monet, but we think he sold that one already to some Panamanian collector.

"That information was from a person who had business in his home here. She recognized the paintings.

"Emanuel the Great comes to town, Rincon has an accident ... you see what I mean? This is number six."

"The lovely Clementine in Chiriqui Grande?"

"A Goya and a Matisse that may be authentic or may not. If it's a copy, it's a damned good one." Willie replied. "This is actually number seven, because of that."

"He doesn't steal the stuff, himself!" Roberto cried. "He leaves it there for us to find! What the *hell* is he up to!? Why?!"

"Shhh!" Willie hissed. "You're getting loud."

He looked around. People were staring. He looked apologetic.

Clint took out his phone and called a friend, Manolo, who was an Interpol agent under cover as a drug supply contact. When he answered Clint said, "Rincon et al."

"Willie and Roberto there?"

"Uh-huh."

"They're a trip! Living in some fantasy world. Probably legit. Found three pieces here, so far. Four, if what I heard last night's up. I'm waiting for information on another one, but won't know until there's an excuse to go into the house."

"Four."

"They follow some nut around. He finds the stuff, I think. They're there for the rewards. Got a bundle."

"Authorized?"

"Yes and no. Used and tolerated to whatever extent seems advisable."

"Thanks."

"A la orden."

Clint hung up and sat back. "Fair enough. I don't think Emanuel is a killer. I just can't see it."

Willie nodded and said, "But seven ain't no coincidence."

"There is that. I'll see what I can find. I want a couple of answers."

He looked around the restaurant, shrugged, and said, "I'll be in contact, probably."

He gulped down the last of his coffee and got up to go outside. He saw someone who shouldn't be there.

Maybe those two characters weren't the only ones following Emanuel around – but to what end? What was there about this one that Clint recognized? He looked like a normal Panamanian with a Latin parent and a gringo or European parent. There were a lot of the mix around. Why did Clint feel there was something about him that meant he shouldn't be there? So far as he could tell, he'd never seen him before.

Clint studied him a moment before he went to where he could be seen. Even from fifty feet away, the bright blue eyes stood out. This one was very good with disguises. If Clint hadn't seen those eyes on the bus he wouldn't have known it was the same person.

On the bus. In Chiriqui Grande. He must have been the stranger at Rio Uyama. Maybe there would be a few puzzles mixed in with a few more in this mess!

Clint wanted to find out something about that one. He didn't have any way, except to follow him to where he could get the information. He wished Judi was there. She was a genius for getting information!

Clint went to the police station, to find that Rincon's car was about half a kilometer back along the road from where he was found, inside a fence that enclosed land he owned. It had a flat tire and he carried no spare. He had, apparently, been inspecting the property and had returned to his car to discover the flat. He decided to walk the distance to town to have someone go to repair the tire and had been struck by some vehicle that didn't bother to stop, fearing trouble with the law. Possibly drinking, or something. There was a fifty-fifty chance they would find the vehicle that killed him.

Clint nodded, but he doubted very much that anything would ever be found. He asked if Julio could find out anything about the mysterious stranger with the very blue eyes. Julio said he could, very easily.

Clint decided to find Emanuel, if he could. He strolled around the town and mentioned him to various people. A woman who worked at the bus terminal said he was probably the one who left very early. She remembered him because he was staying so carefully out of sight of the others at the station. He took a bus to Darien.

Would that mean Clint went to Darien now? Why not? He wanted to see as much of the country as he could.

He went back to the police station. Julio said the man he asked about had bought a bus ticket to Darien. His name, on his passport, was Arnaldo Valenz from Colombia. He was a tourist visiting friends.

"Which bus?" Clint asked.

"The one that leaves in about an hour."

So. Emanuel takes a bus in the morning and Arnaldo takes one in the early afternoon for the same place. What was the connection? Nothing made any sense. It didn't even seem possible.

Of course, he could have found that Emanuel took the early bus the same way Clint did.

Clint called Manolo again and asked if the name 'Castile' meant anything. He said, if it was the one between Bocas and Chiriqui Grande, there was a question about a painting. He got it legit, but they wanted to know the seller.

"Rincon," Clint answered. Manolo said that was a suspicion. So. Now he would definitely go to Darien.

Clint saved the price of a bus ticket. He called Roberto and said their quarry was on his way to Darien. If they were going he would appreciate a ride with them. He was doing all this at his own expense.

Half an hour later they left for Darien.

They came into the lush Darien area late enough that they wouldn't be able to find anything that night. Clint stayed in a different hotel than Willie and Roberto. It might be a good idea that people didn't connect them. They agreed. Clint meshed with people anywhere, they never did.

"I dress and act like them. You don't. Think about it."

During the drive Clint found they weren't so bad. They just lived in some silly fantasy world they'd learned, as Emanuel said, from movies, TV, and bad rap garbage. Willie gave a sickly grin. Roberto laughed and said he'd change when this act didn't work anymore. Clint resisted saying it wasn't working now. Like Dave said to that idiot with the loud speakers in his car, "News flash! It's not WORK-K-K-KING!"

Clint asked the girl in the bus station restaurant about Emanuel. The bus wouldn't be there for another hour and a half or so. It stopped for half an hour, twice, along the way, and he'd have to transfer in the last one.

The area was beautiful, but most of Panamá is. Clint could picture Dave there with his camera and troop of local Indios. He would be there half an hour and have pictures of twenty species that weren't supposed to be found in Panamá.

He'd said the area was explored. Probably no more than five new species. Clint grinned to himself and found a good restaurant. Willie and Roberto would, no doubt, be waiting there when Emanuel got off the bus. So would Clint, but he wouldn't follow Emanuel. Those two clowns wouldn't actually bother Emanuel. They wanted to be where he was so they could collect the bounty on the missing art. Clint was surprised that so much of it was in Panamá, but knew it was from his work with Manolo.

The bus came. Emanuel didn't come with it. Neither did Arnaldo. Willie and Roberto were running around, loudly demanding to know where Emanuel got off. No one knew anything.

Clint leaned against the side of the bus where the door boy was getting the luggage out of the compartment. Willie and Roberto were running around, asking anyone who got off if they'd seen the weird preacher.

"I don't know if they're funny or just pathetic," Clint said conversationally to the boy, who gave him a big grin. They'd tried to stop him for answers when he came to get the bags.

"Locos. Officiales. Fuck them!"

"They just say they're officials. They're mostly wannabe badasses, I think."

"All they have to do is say, 'I'm looking for a man who was supposed to be on your bus, but may have missed it, or something,' and I'd tell them he and three other people got off at Vilas Pendros. Now, fuck them!"

"Some people never learn."

"They watch too much television. Fuck them!"

Clint saluted and went into the little restaurant. Willie and Roberto came in twenty minutes later.

"They all refuse to say anything at all to us!" Willie complained. "We'll have to go back along the road the bus came and check every damned stop along the way!"

"I think I'll go out to the Vilas," Clint sad. "He got off there."

Roberto dropped his coffee all over his lap. Willie knocked the silverware off the table when he spun to goggle at Clint.

"When ... how did you find out!?" Roberto cried.

"When the bus stopped. I asked a woman if my nephew, the thin tired and sour-looking gringo, got off before he got here – like he was prone to do. She said he was probably one of the people who got off at the vilas."

"But they wouldn't tell us anything!" Willie complained.

"They wouldn't tell some stupid TV asshole cops any-thing. Try just asking in a polite way what you want to know. Demand answers from these people and one thing is damned certain – you won't be getting any. If you do, they won't be right."

"Jesus!" Roberto said. "All this time we could be ... where are these vilas?"

"Maybe fifteen kilometers back."

"Want a ride?"

"No. He won't be there."

"He won't?"

"I seriously doubt he would be there. He could figure you'd find where he was headed and would manage to have you here waiting for him for enough time to do whatever he wanted to do."

"We have to check, anyhow."

"See you around." They left. Clint grinned and ordered another empanada and another cup of coffee.

The local bus came in just three minutes after Willie and Roberto ran to their car and almost had a head-on leaving the parking lot. Clint waited until the passengers were mostly out to walk up to Emanuel and say, "Hello!"

Emanuel grinned at him. "You figured I'd fool them into

going somewhere else. I don't know what they want, but I know they are probably dangerous. I do not think they are, shall we say, the brightest flowers in the vase.

"It is good to see you, Clint. You are following me too? Why?"

"Not you," Clint replied. "One of the people who're following you."

"Dear lord! How many are following me, and *why* are they following me?"

"As to how many, I can't say. As to why, you lead them to other things they're after."

He looked serious. "I know of only those two. I have made it a game to outsmart them. I do not know why *they* are following me."

Clint nodded. "What do you base your stops on?"

"People and places I hear about through my personal correspondence. Computer, you see."

"You don't carry one."

"There are cafés everywhere. Internet services, even in the jungles. The modern world."

Clint agreed. "So. Someone is sending you to specific places for specific reasons. You're then leading someone else, probably someone in on it, to very specific people. This sounds like some silly TV show.

"Emanuel, who's doing this to you?"

"Doing *what*?! I am confused."

"Let's go somewhere and try to figure this thing out. Make it look like you're going to the restroom or some-thing. Meet me later somewhere. *Do not* go to wherever you're supposed to go here!"

He nodded and said he was going to look for a hotel or pension. He was supposed to contact someone named

Marta Rosadas Javier.

Clint said to move around a bit, then jump on the bus to the vilas down the street. Flag it down near the turnoff road..

Emanuel grinned and said he liked this part where he got to outsmart someone he never even knew was there.

Clint got up, saluted, paid his tab, and walked out. There was a bus to the vilas every hour. He made it a point to be on the next one. Emanuel was walking along the road, just past the turnoff, and flagged the bus. He came to sit next to Clint.

Clint watched the road behind. About half a mile from the town he called "Sparate!" and they got off. They were around a bend and Clint pulled Emanuel into the trees by the road. A taxi came by less than half a minute later, going toward the vilas.

Clint grinned at Emanuel, who looked excited.

"We're on the next one to Panamá City.. It'll be about ... it's four fifteen. It won't be until a bit after eight. We can try to figure this out, in the meantime," Clint said. "Did you know there's a murder or two everywhere you go?"

"*Murder*?!?!"

"The people you contact are, so far as I can determine, art thieves and fences. You're being used to ... what's the matter?"

"I knew there were an inordinate amount of accidents and so forth. I didn't know there were any *murders*! I was beginning to become somewhat suspicious, but nothing happened after I met you. I feel you are a good luck charm, though I do not believe in such things. That smacks to me of witchcraft."

"Who directs you to these people?"

"It is a woman in the missionary council. Veronica Leona Messer. She is in charge of international affairs."

"Oh? Your church is large enough to have an international council?!"

"No, no! It is an international institution who make no judgements about the church. They merely aid in placing missionaries into contact with people and places that are in great need of enlighten ... they are a purely non-denominational charity service. It is the Name Supreme International Aid Society."

"They contacted you when you began this trip?"

"Well, yes. I had spoken with a man who aided me greatly in my quest. He recommended that I cooperate as much as possible with the service because they were known to do great work without making judgements. They are interested in aiding people in any way they can arrange."

"Well, a minimum of three people have had accidents that weren't accidents since I met you. In Bocas and in Las Tablas."

"I did not know about this! I swear by all that is holy! I would never be any small part of harming anyone!" If he wasn't one hell of an actor he was totally devastated by this news.

"Well, we can make ourselves comfortable. I want to know a bit more about this council thing. Someone's using it for reasons diametrically opposed to its purpose.

"How do they work it? They obviously know where you're going and who you contact."

"No, no. They give me the name and what information they can. I have a knack for finding people. I have failed to find only four or five since my quest ... since my trip began. I speak with people in a given small area. I have some information that will make people remember something, if you understand."

They talked awhile. Clint called Manolo to get any information he could find about the council. Judging from the way those two clowns acted it was no surprise they couldn't locate people. Even if they were standing dead in front of the person they wouldn't get information.

Clint and Emanuel walked back toward the town and waited in a restaurant not far from the bus stop until it was loading the few people who were boarding this early in the trip. There were only four. Clint and Emanuel ran to the bus as it was in motion to leave and climbed aboard. Clint greeted the people already aboard and chatted a moment with all of them. It was two men and their wives.

On the trip to Panamá City, Clint made it a point to be where he could observe everyone who got on the bus. The one he half-expected didn't board the bus.

He and Emanuel made an arrangement to get the next predetermined stop set up. Emanuel wouldn't countenance lying so Clint said he wouldn't be lying. He would simply say that he left Darien because some people who seemed dangerous to him were there. That was true.

In Panamá City, they went to an internet café, where he got the next destination. The woman, Veronica, seemed very distressed that anyone was following him. She just couldn't imagine why anyone would be interested in a missionary who was there to aid the needy.

They found an out-of-the-way moderate hotel in a dangerous section of the city. Clint would go everywhere with Emanuel until they left. For Bocas Town. Home.

Clint and Emanuel got off the Bocas del Toro bus at Valle de Aguas at 8:10 in the morning. Clint called Judi and said they were coming. He called Manolo as soon as they were settled in.

"Clint, there isn't much I can find out about that council. It's registered by a ... CIA front, if you want the truth. There are ties with Interpol et al. I do some work with them. I don't pretend to like the implications. At all."

"There has to be something else. A better reason."

"I'm digging. I've always said the methods used by the CIA stink. They and DEA are worse than most of the ones they catch. 'The end justifies the means' is a pile of horseshit. You know I won't go along with a lot of it."

"I think I know what they'll claim. It'll be another pile of horseshit. Thanks, Manolo."

Okay. Clint figured it was the CIA and that they'd claim the profits from the sale of the stolen art was financing terrorism. That was certainly on the minds of Willie and Roberto. All they were doing was seeing that these people were stopped in any way they could. No one was dead who deserved to live.

Maybe. What about that snakebite victim? What did she have to do with it? Was she just in the way? Using someone like Emanuel, who, despite the fact he was irritating and a bit obnoxious at first, was innocent was the inexcusable part. He was a person who cared about other people. That was the totally inescapable fact. They could play all the games they wanted. Both sides – but only so long as they left innocent people out of it. Involving such people crossed the line, a long way. Clint wasn't the least hesitant about setting certain types against each other. It saved decent taxpayers a bundle for one or fifty of them to knock off one or fifty others. They didn't have to spend a million bucks apiece a year keeping them locked up.

The Robinson Emanuel was supposed to locate was here. Here or close.

Why did they need Emanuel?

Because it was a very large family. There were a number of them who might be involved in art theft. There weren't any, so far as Clint knew, who would be involved with terrorists, in any way. Finding one certain individual in that family would be one hell of a hard task. They would protect one another, and would put out a lot of false information. The one they were after would probably be very popular among a large group. The family was deeply involved in politics and knew how to manipulate people.

Emanuel would lay low awhile, until they found out a few things about the followers.

Judi came home from shopping about four o'clock and told Clint Willie and Roberto were back. Would Emanuel be the reason?

"They asked, in their own charming inimitable way, if you were here. I said I couldn't say. You weren't here last night."

"If they ask again, just say I came in, am in a very bad mood and keep ranting about people screwing with my mind."

She smirked at him. "So. How are the DEA and CIA mixed up in this?"

Clint giggled. She got that information in two minutes, probably.

"That's what I can't quite figure. They're very definitely involved, but there's one other I can't figure from any angle.

"You know something else? I think Willie and Roberto don't have a clue about him! *He's* why they keep running into dead ends!"

"Who?"

"Don't I wish I knew the real answer to that."

She laughed and said she would go on home. If they were watching they would know she came there.

Sure enough. As soon as she went home they called to ask if Clint was back yet.

"He's back, and in a horrible mood! I don't know what happened, but I damned well intend to keep away from him until he cools down! What a mood!"

"Is anyone with him? We heard he came in with someone. A man."

"I didn't see anyone. He may have stashed a guest somewhere, probably in Almirante or Changuinola. It could be why he's in such a bad mood. Someone imposing on him makes him, shall we say, a bit irate."

She was playing the airheaded ditzo. They would figure she didn't know anything and that they could use her to get information.

Hah! She could play them like a Stradivarius!

They soon said goodbye and hung up. It wouldn't occur to them that she stalked out in Chiriqui Grande because she thought they were the lowest kind of scum?

Probably not. They got a lot of that.

Clint thought for a few minutes, then called Manny Mathews, a retired mafia don from the states living in the area to avoid his old life and raise a family who wouldn't be ashamed of how pops made his. He and Clint, who arranged the retirement, were close friends. He still had ways to get information that were far above anything else.

Clint asked which Robinson had stolen art. Manny said he'd call back in fifteen minutes. When he did, he started with, "Two of them. Yveth and Fabio. Here and in Changuinola. Also a Taylor and an Arauz are into collecting such items."

They chatted for a few minutes, then Clint went to Emanuel to ask if he knew which Robinson he was after.

"I'm not yet certain. I have to ... I would have to meet them to determine which one. I know a little about her to make the connection, you see. I would tell her that Beth Chandler, from San Diego, said to drop by if I was in the area. That is true – according to Veronica."

Clint nodded and said he could probably determine it was an Yveth.

"Contact Veronica and tell her you couldn't deliver the message because Yveth is the only one it could be, and she's not here for another two weeks. She's in Costa Rica, visiting a cousin."

"I can't say that!"

"Why not? It's true."

"Oh. You checked and found that out. You are not asking that I prevaricate. I see."

Clint nodded. Maybe Emanuel wouldn't lie about anything. He would!

An hour later, after spending the time on the computer e-mailing a number of his friends, Emanuel said that Veronica suggested he go to Panamá City to see if he could aid a Fernando Harris D'Angona. The man was in spiritual crisis, and would be able to fund a clinic if he could be convinced that it would assuage his soul of past mistakes. He was using another name, but he would know Norman Donaldson, from Atlanta, Georgia, USA. Use the name to help convince Mr. Harris of the sincerity of wanting to help him find the true blah, blah, blah.

Clint sighed. He called Air Panamá to book them on the morning flight. They would be damned sure no one knew about that trip. Clint had worked with the police here on several cases, and they had strict instructions about what might happen if anyone let out information concerning Clint Faraday and anyone working with him.

Clint decided not to go to town that night. It would be in character for him to stay home if he was in a bad mood. He would never take a bad mood out at night.

He got a good night's sleep. He and Emanuel (in enough of a disguise that he might not be recognized by anyone who didn't already know him) got to the plane at the last moment and went aboard. Clint studied the other passengers by going along the aisle before takeoff to say "Hello!" to all he knew. Judi would tell Willie and Roberto that Clint and some friend from the states went to Panamá City on the early flight.

Clint felt that Emanuel was having more excitement and fun from all this crap than he ever knew before in his life.

They landed at Tocumen, where Clint called Jerry Ames, a friend who had a condo in the city, to have him and Emanuel picked up and taken somewhere where Emanuel wouldn't be found. Clint would stay at the Hotel California, as usual.

Next step was to contact the police there. He had worked with them on several cases and had established a reputation of being honest and practical, as well as a person who had a good slant on many things.

"Fernando Harris D'Angona. A contact name to identify him is Norman Donaldson from Atlanta, Georgia. I don't think they have any idea what name he's using here. Something about Emanuel would make him come out of the woodwork, so to speak."

Oscar Pinela nodded. "I think I know, within ten people, who you seek. I don't know why you think he would have an accident if he's located."

"There's a long history of people contacted by Emanuel who have fatal accidents within hours." Clint told him about a few.

"And you say he isn't responsible, that he is being used?"

"I'm fairly certain of it. I could be wrong, but he's a better actor than anyone in the flicks or on TV if he's doing any of it."

He nodded again. "What kind of thing connects the victims?"

"Stolen art."

"Then it will be Rodrigo Lordes, Francisco Dariez, Flaco

Gorda, or Jorge Maestro. They are the only ones who are rich enough or who have the necessary contacts to locate such things. They are the only ones using an alias here. We watch such people without letting them know we are aware they are not who their identification says they are."

"Flaco Gorda?" ("Skinny Fat?")

He shrugged.

Clint found the places he might run into the four and went out. The closest place was the Rosa de la Noche, a legal house of prostitution. Francisco Dariez often came in, but after eight at night.

The Top Place Billiares # something-or-other was next. Rodrigo Lordes was playing eight ball for a dollar a ball. Clint bought in and played a couple of games, winning four dollars on one and seven on the next. He mentioned a man named Norman Donaldson, in Atlanta, Georgia, knew some people who played pool very well here. He told Clint about it a while before Clint moved to Panamá.

"I think I do not play pool so very well!" he cried.

"Oh, I know the game. Norm said I'd find a challenge here. You're a lot better than most. I just sort of have a natural talent for it."

He grinned and bought them both beers. He said he knew the hustling game. Clint was good at it.

"Got to eat!" Clint agreed. He laughed and said playing against Clint was a good way to end up starving.

The next place was dominoes, which Clint wasn't at all good at. He watched them play for a few minutes and stood at the bar when Flaco Gorda came to get another beer. He wasn't flaco (skinny) or gordo (fat). He was fairly well constructed, in a slightly less than bullish way.

Clint asked if he knew anyone in the states. Georgia.

"A couple," he replied, in very good English. "I spent two years there. Came home last year. You can have the states."

"I thought I saw you there! You were with that Norman character!"

"Norm Donaldson? He's, as you say there, quite the trip, isn't he?"

"Good for business contacts, though," Clint said.

He got a studied look, then a small grin. "I would never figure you for the type who collects antiques."

"I work for someone who does. I couldn't care less about art. Take a photo of anything with a ten megapixel camera and save the canvas and paint. Lasts forever, and doesn't fade and chip so you gotta spend a grand having it cleaned. Print out fifty copies anytime you want."

He laughed. "You can't get the handwork that way, but I agree. Spend the dough on something you like. It's investment. Something for the grandkids."

"That's about as soon as you can cash in that CD!"

He laughed again and said he had to get back in the game. His luck was about to change. He could always feel it.

So. He was as good as Emanuel for locating these people. He would contact Manolo and get the next on the list.. According to Emanuel, they said there were about ten people who needed their attention. Emanuel was getting a bit turned off by these people and the way they were using him.

He went back to the hotel and told Emanuel to e-mail Veronica and tell her D'Angona was using the name Flaco Gorda and was a deeply troubled soul who hid his shame behind a facade of what looked like a somewhat swollen ego.

"He will be safe?"

Clint shrugged. He said it was likely he would be protected, but he wasn't responsible for what happened to those people. They knew the rules when they forced themselves into the game.

Emanuel looked worried. Clint said the object of the locating was taken away now, but no one knew that. He was fairly certain there was plenty of time to make Flaco Gordo reasonably safe from anything except the law. He was a dealer in stolen property.

They went out to a good restaurant. Clint got a disapproving look when he ordered a beer. He said the Bible taught moderation, temperance, not abstinence. He thought about it for a minute, said he'd never tasted beer, and ordered one.

He didn't like the taste, so Clint ordered a red wine for him. He sipped it, said it wasn't much better, then said it had a sort of nice aftertaste, didn't it?

"The good ones do. This is one to make a meal more pleasant. The cheap ones are to get drunk. I very seldom allow myself to get drunk."

"Please see to it that I practice temperance and don't get drunk."

The night was rather pleasant. Emanuel wasn't half bad when he dropped the religious part. Before the night was through he said maybe he was beginning to see how people saw him. He was a royal pain in the ass, wasn't he?

"Not nearly as bad as some. Tonight, you're a good companion."

They turned in fairly early.

In the morning the phone woke him at four forty two. It

was Oscar.

"Flaco Gorda? He was the one?" he said when Clint answered.

"Yeah. He ... *was* the one?"

"He had a bit of an accident. Got drunk and fell into an already broken plate glass window. It cut his throat almost professionally."

"When? And where?"

"About an hour ago. Near the causeway."

"Will it get any publicity?"

"I do not believe it will. He was not that important and was not well known."

"Good. I have to check some things and it might be a great help if no one knows he's dead."

"I see. Someone you suspect will say the wrong thing to show he knows things he can't know except one way."

They talked for a minute. Clint went to check Emanuel's room. The causeway was far enough away that he couldn't very well get back in an hour. He would definitely not use a taxi who might remember him.

He was there, and sleeping. Clint said he always forgot that most people didn't get up when he did. He apologized for waking him and went down to the restaurant – that wouldn't open before six thirty.

That gave him an idea. To get in before six thirty you had to ring for the clerk to buzz the lock open to the door. No one had left after two ten AM and no one had come in since then, either.

Clint went out and to an all-night restaurant for a fairly decent breakfast. He went back to the hotel at seven thirty and called Emanuel, who said he was up. That was the time he got up every morning. He came down and they went to another restaurant. Clint had coffee and a slice of melon. Emanuel had an omelet and orange juice. Then they went to the internet café not far away.

"Veronica said she was glad I got to speak with D'Angona, and was he among those they could hope to salvage?" Emanuel reported. "I said we do what we can. Some people can be most difficult, but there is always hope. I think we managed to reach him enough that we may be successful in saving him from damnation.

"She said, if I could squeeze in the time and it won't be too much of an inconvenience, could I go to a place in Bocas del Toro called Mali. Do you know it?

"I told her it was never inconvenient to help show the path to another lost soul.

"I sound obsequious to myself! Great lord!"

Clint laughed. "You want the truth? You look actually human this morning."

He reached to touch Clint's hand. That said it all.

"Who and how? Mali?"

"Oh. Virgil Patterson. A woman he knew in the states, Nancy Killian Moore, recommended I contact him. She doesn't know why he would change his name, but he did. She has become very worried that he had gone far astray down here."

"In these dangerous savage pagan lands," Clint finished. Emanuel looked a bit shocked, then a slow grin spread over his face. He gave Clint the bird, though he didn't quite get it right. It wasn't a thing he'd used before.

"You know something? I think I can be normal ... well, what will pass as normal. All I have to do is 'loosen up,' as they say."

Clint agreed. "I have an errand to run while I'm here. We

can get a bus to Mali at eight. I'll be out there so I'll get the tickets."

"I think I want to see the city through open eyes. Eyes that aren't clouded with preconceived ideas. I really do like the Panamanian people. I'll feel a little guilty. The council is paying my way so I told Veronica that I was out of funds and going so far was costing much more than I anticipated. She will send me five hundred dollars by Western Union. It will be there before three o'clock."

Clint agreed to be back by six thirty. They could get a good meal and make the bus. They would get to Mali at about seven thirty in the morning. Clint went to the police station for a report, but there wasn't anything more. He thought a bit, then went to the station to get tickets for Bocas del Toro. He didn't doubt a certain blue-eyed individual would be on that bus.

They arrived in Mali at seven thirty four. Only Clint and Emanuel got off the bus. No one on the bus could be the blue-eyed follower.

Clint knew how he was disguised. Three people got off the bus in Chiriqui, at the bombas. The Changuinola bus picked up riders there. The three were surfer types, and were speaking German. They seemed to be together, but Clint noticed that one had his bags with him inside the bus, a couple of small backpacks. The others had their surfboards that had to be unloaded from the compartment. The third one hung around like he was with them, but walked across to the new Shell station while the other two went towards the David casita. He would definitely be on the Changuinola-David bus. Clint wondered if he would change the disguise or figure he wasn't noticed. Mali is small. Just a puebla. It would be very difficult to not be noticed there. It was something that Emanuel could use to locate Virgil quickly.

What did Virgil look like? Did Emanuel know?

"No. He is average and dark enough that he could pass as a mestizo. Veronica says he has a knack for languages so may speak very good Spanish. He will speak like a native."

"How will you locate him?"

"I will simply ask about people who are too rich and not well-liked. There are seldom more than four or five in a given area. I will mention Nancy Killian Moore where each will hear the name. He will then introduce himself."

Clint nodded. He would leave locating Virgil to Emanuel

while he went on to the next stop to wait until the follower got off the bus there. He definitely wouldn't get off at the previous stop. There would be no way he wouldn't be noticed. A surfer might get off ... at the restaurant where the bus stopped for ten minutes for people to use the restrooms or whatever. Clint would be there to greet him. He wanted to know what this was about. It wasn't someone looking for stolen art or bounty hunting. There was something a lot deeper than that.

He grabbed a passing taxi and headed for the restaurant. The bus came about a quarter hour later. The surfer got off and paid his fare, while explaining that a friend was going to pick him up there. Clint waited until he headed for the restrooms and followed him in. He went into a booth, stayed about eight minutes and a totally different type of person came out. The bus had just left. No one would notice.

Clint damned well did!

The man, now looking like a native, probably a cattle man, strolled out toward the road to hail a cab. Clint waited and jumped aboard as it started off.

"Hi. Clint Faraday, here with Emanuel, as you know."

The fellow laughed. "I thought you made me back in David, and again in Chiriqui Grande. I'm Raul Santana, at the moment."

"What the hell is this about? Why use someone like Emanuel?"

"It's big. Really big.

"I like the way you ran Willie and Berto around! You had them take you to Darien – so why didn't you take the ride back when they ... because it wasn't done yet. I'm dead tired."

He called for the taxi to stop, and they got out. He said he was paranoid about talking anywhere they might be heard. Mali was about twenty minutes walking. They walked on.

"Is Interpol involved?"

"Not on my end. I'm working for a sort of government. Interpol couldn't begin to afford me. They have what we call a limited budget. I let Willie and Berto collect on that arty stuff from the insurance companies. They're comic relief to me.

"I did a pretty fair check on you. Did you really get fees on the order of my own? Two mil for that land scam in Puerto Armuelles?"

"Well, the hospital and clinic got the fees. I just keep enough to live on – and to run all over hell and back on things like this. I'm not hurting. Definitely."

"I think I'm going to retire, soon. I can't spend ten percent of what I make. I'm like you in that I do it because somebody has to eliminate some of the worst and most dangerous people in the world."

"Art thieves? Worst and most dangerous?"

"If that was all, I wouldn't waste my time. I'm trying to cut a cancer out that was growing far too fast, now it's being excised."

"You going to tell me what it's about?"

"Remember the nuclear crap with that weird group in California?"

"No connection. I know that."

"No *direct* connection. The connection is on the supply end. The aim is to remove a certain couple of countries from ever again running the world through a lot of contrived incidents and so forth. Believe it or not, they financed the original part of this and now are paying me to try to clean up the mess they've made of things."

"It's getting away from them now? They only thought they were in charge?"

"Something like that. They were going to corner the nuclear crap and hold it over the heads of anyone who didn't agree to their concept of a perfect world – which consists, of course, of them having all the power and privilege. It seems they were able to get a group together to steal the art – and a lot of things with more real and intrinsic value – and use it to finance the venture. The group who hold the art have gotten together here, Colombia, Venezuela, and Mexico and made a plan to do exactly what was planned, with one small difference."

"They would have the power and privilege."

"Uh-huh. This one, nobody wins. I've managed to stop the possible supply, now I'm eliminating the ones who were making the plans."

"It seems to me you're working for the original planners. A, as you say, minor detail."

"They think so, too.

"Clint, these people chose Panamá to hide. Two of them are from here, and some have spent time here. They're concentrated here, but one is here and one is there in three other countries. I don't know why they aren't mostly in their original base country."

"Because, why would they be here? There's also that the location's central and they have the canal they can use to come and go without being particularly noted. It's a paradise country where they can go into small towns and live a great life. The thing that catches them and sets them off from the natives is that they're the type they are. Those people aren't liked by anyone, anywhere. They don't see it.

"The difference here and in the more socalled modern and sophisticated places is that the natives will pity them and the city people will play them for what they can get. They never seem to catch on that they're really a pathetic bunch of cruds. They think they're impressing people with what they have. They don't realize they don't have anything these people want.

"Don't use Emanuel anymore, Okay?"

"It's almost done. There are two more here. Emanuel has an amazing ability for finding them. I don't know where he gets the information."

"Veronica."

"The one he e-mails? She can give him enough information that he can find them in no time, yet she doesn't do it herself?"

"It's a very simple system. You get all the modern techniques and such and get nowhere. He ... it doesn't matter. He has a knack. It probably wouldn't work for us.

"You know damned well I can't give strong circumstantial evidence to get you, don't you."

"That's why I can command such ridiculous fees. We won't hurt Emanuel."

"I wouldn't give a damn if it was only the guilty. What about that girl and the snakebite?"

"That was a snakebite, believe it or not. I only went there because people said Castile was a friend of Rincon. She was fine when I left. She was trying to get me into bed, probably for a fee, but I didn't have the time. I think it would have been fun."

Clint thought and nodded.

"The rest are the original planners?"

"Yes. For the most part. I know who they are. Emanuel's job is almost done."

"Many of them?"

"Right now, four in this area. They think they're totally safe."

"Nobody is."

"True. Watch your back, Clint. If they tumble that you know anything you have to remember you're no more safe than they are."

"I won't go after you, you won't go after me. We understand what the hell is going on in the world. Just be absolutely sure no innocent friend of mine gets drawn into it."

"I like the Indios, too. They treat me like I'm just another person who may be interesting and maybe even could be a friend. That wouldn't change if they knew what I'm doing, would it?"

"They might not approve, but they wouldn't make judgements so long as you don't involve them or their people."

"Just like you. And me."

Clint nodded.

"Who? Here?"

Clint considered. "I think I know! I wonder ... can Emanuel find this one?"

"You can, it would seem."

"If I know what I'm looking for. I could ask the Indios in this kind of place about certain things and know in minutes.

"No. I won't ."

He laughed. "I didn't think you would. It's my gig, not

yours."

"But I won't protect them, either."

He grinned. They came on a group of Indios waiting for a bus. The small children ran out to hug Clint. He embraced a couple of the adults and chatted a minute. He introduced Raul and said, very frankly, that it wasn't his real name. They accepted that and included him in the conversation.

They walked on and into the small collection of homes near the little store. Emanuel was there and said that Ernesto Lopez was out riding somewhere and wouldn't be back until late. He left a note that he had called and would possibly come back next week if he was in the area.

"You aren't going to wait for him here?" Clint asked.

"No. His girlfriend says he sometimes stays for three or four days when he rides out with those two snobs from Panamá City, so I'll go on. From what she said and what others said I doubt I could reach the poor soul. They say he is entirely obsessed with money and thinks he's the king of the world. They say he is a very sad and unhappy man and that makes him a mean and evil man. He blasphemes constantly, and says – this is what they say he says, not my words – `God can kiss my ass.' That is so sad. I believe him to be damned beyond redemption, though I feel God will forgive anything if there is true remorse.

"I am torn. I may be able to help the man, but it may not be possible. I am not the best at reaching such people."

"Well, I always felt you took such things too personally. You can only try. It's not your fault if they're so set in their ways they won't listen to anyone else.

"There! I've come around a bit toward your philosophy!

You're getting to me!"

Emanuel laughed. "You're not a very good liar, Clint. I think there's hope."

"Where will we go next?" Clint asked. "Raul" said he had to move on. He had an important meeting. He shook hands with Emanuel and Clint and strolled on toward the south along the road.

"I will contact Veronica when we are back in David. I would like to take the bus to the dam and get off there. I want to look around the area where you gave me such insight into my own mind and brought my hidden fears into the light.

"Clint. I want to walk out on that dam and look at the beautiful scene on both sides. I want to look down to that river, hundreds of meters below, and feel the thrill I felt at the washout. I will then flag the next bus into David.

"Clint, I am most serious. You have freed me.

"I will, of course, continue on my quest for Veronica and the group. I gave my word. I never do that lightly. I will also inform her that I feel it is fast coming the time I will seek other ways to help my fellow man. I feel the path chosen is not effective enough.

"I will find a place. Perhaps here in Panamá. I think Darien was beautiful and natural.

"Clint, I am not going to try to impress anyone with my beliefs anymore. That was a terrible mistake, and had the result of turning people away from me and from God. I did not see it.

"I will be like Alan, the man who took me in and saved me from the horrors my parents' sad lifestyle can engender. I will let there be no mistakes in thinking I am not a very religious person, but I will offer advice only when asked. I will not volunteer that advice unless it is a case such as these for Veronica, and I will not try to force anyone to accept my word. I have learned that lesson. I am as capable of being wrong as anyone else."

Clint nodded. They waited a few minutes and boarded the next bus. They got off at the dam. Emanuel walked shakily out a short distance on the reservoir side, and stood to scan the area. He took out a digital camera and took some photos, then walked across to the drop and river side. Clint, waiting for him at the end of the dam, could see he was shaking and almost terrified, but he went and looked out, then down. He stood for a moment, then took some pictures, then went out farther and repeated the ritual.

He came back, walking steadily. His eyes were almost in a fanatic gleam. "It's truly magnificent! What hath God wrought!

"Clint! I am *free*!"

He hugged Clint tightly. Clint was surprised, and didn't quite know how to react.

"Shall we continue to David?" Emanuel asked happily.

They waited at the line of small stores by the road. Emanuel went out to the little rise at the reception center and took some more pictures. The next bus was full, so they took the following one. They got into David at dusk.

Clint took Emanuel to the Pension Costa Rica and got them both rooms. He went to Peter's for awhile, then to Bohmfalk's, then returned for the night. Emanuel had gone to the internet and contacted Veronica. She said she had only one other for him to contact now. A woman in San Blas. She, like so many lost souls, was using an alias there, but would know the name Daniela Winston. She liked horses, and was known to be somewhere in that area. Emanuel said he told her that would work out exceptionally well, as he was planning on staying in Panamá. He felt he could do some real good here, but working with medical and educational projects that didn't include religion directly.

"I told her I am through being some kind of evangelical closed-minded preacher out to save the world from itself. She said she wished me well and that she would send ten thousand dollars to help me get started in good works.

"I replied that the fund surely wasn't enough for such a hit, but she said there was a special fund to help those who found where their real calling was. She, quite frankly, was never convinced that the methods we were using were effective. Help in areas that met a true and deep need of the local people are effective. She said she is always uneasy about methods that are like hitting people in the head with a board to make them see the light. It, too often, results in their losing sight of the light altogether.

"I never knew her to be so practical, but I suppose she is in a position where she must follow rules of others to be able to accomplish any good at all. I believe her to be a very good person."

Clint didn't say what he felt about the lovely Veronica. He managed a nod. Tomorrow, Emanuel would go to San Blas.

In the morning Clint went with Emanuel to the bus station, where he sent him off. He would e-mail Clint about his projects from time-to-time. Clint went to La Tipica for breakfast. He talked with a lot of friends from the area and caught up on the latest gossip. About ten o'clock he was back at the Costa Rica to collect his things . He would take a later bus to Bocas del Toro and home.

He saw a sort of dumpy character sitting on a rocking chair in the front of the pension simply because he always automatically noted everyone in such places. He got his bags and was heading out. He glanced at the old fellow and noted the startling blue eyes.

He grinned and waved. "Raul" laughed and came to walk with him.

"I'm called Chico now," he said, putting on his dark sunglasses. "I think there's little for me to do anymore. The Panamá part is as much as done.

"One left. You gonna tell me where or do I have to spend twenty minutes finding out my own way?"

"San Blas. What about the fine upstanding Mr. Lopez?"

"I'm afraid Mr. Lopez, Miss Garcia, and Mr. Williams rode out from a little burg called Mali to a place in some area called Bajo El Valle and got caught in a little rockslide. Three hundred meters into the rocks by the river. Sad.

"I said four. One more, in Panamá, then back to the states. My job'll be done in about a month, then I retire. I wish there was a way I could come here and not be found. I don't know what it is about this country, but you start to think in an entirely different way here. I would like to spend the next fifty years in Panamá, I think."

"There's a way."

"Marko? I knew about that before they moved here. When he was starting to build that place on Isla San Cristobal."

"Marko had to be taught how to disappear. You don't."

"Clint, no matter how good you are at what you do, there's always someone better."

"But does it matter if anyone at that level in your profession knows?"

He thought a moment. "It could be worth a shot! I love this place and these people."

Clint wished him luck. "Take care."

"I always do. I wouldn't survive a day if I didn't."

Clint caught the bus to Bocas del Toro. He was in Chiriqui Grande four hours later, so stayed the night there. He decided to go to Cusapin for a couple of days, called Judi – who said Dave was out there – and got caught up on local affairs, then met Andres at the dock to head for the closest place to paradise he'd ever found.

He got a phone call the third day. The police in David would appreciate it if he would come to make a declaration about several of the things that had happened. They had discovered, through a secret operative for a world-wide policing detail, that several accidental deaths, including the woman in Chiriqui Grande, were non-accidents done by an agent for the very people accused of various conspiracies. The police weren't equipped to handle international intrigue, and wanted it stopped. Clint was their best hope, as the US Embassy claimed no knowledge of any such thing. "A man called Chico Raul is their agent, but we can contact him only in difficult ways. We can't find who he actually is, but he has given much information that fits with the incidents he could only know if he was there.

"He says there was growing suspicion about a man, a missionary, being involved, because more than one accident was at a place and time when he was in the near area, the latest being a woman in San Blas. The agent said it was coincidence, that he was the one who arranged the accidents, that the preacher-man was a good man with a good heart, and even the one who did the acts found it wrong to allow the innocent man to be suspected. None of the victims could be called 'innocent,' in the broadest definition of the word.

"He claimed that the accidents were among a group involved in drug smuggling and art theft, and that he held no sympathy for them.

"We find that the deaths he admitted to did, indeed, involve stolen art. It strengthens his claims. He said you had investigated one or two of the cases – and we have records that you did, indeed, request information about them – and would be able to explain about it."

"I'll come to David and make a declaration, but it's true. It's a war between two opposing groups that could possibly involve the police here and in Colombia and Costa Rica in a very expensive investigation that would, as is usual where those people are involved, result in a bunch of deaths and huge expense that leads to nothing.

"Raul explained it to me. He thinks it's best that they handle it themselves. Dead thugs and drug smugglers don't cost many millions to incarcerate and feed for years. This way, even their own group has to pay for their own funerals."

"You're a very practical man, Clint Faraday. You could have stopped it, but found this is a better way for all concerned."

"I don't think I could have stopped it. I could have caused publicity that would lead to the huge expenses and hopeless prosecution of that bunch of hoods."

"Thank you. I will have this written and you may read it over and use it for your declaration. I will, I assure you, not include certain parts. It will appear you knew nothing, only had suspicions until it was done. Raul has assured us that the project is completed in Panamá. He is now in Colombia, and will thence return to Germany where the, as he named it, cleanup started."

Clint chatted a minute, then made arrangements to return to Chiriqui Grande the following day.

He went fishing. The next day he went to David. The next day he went to Bocas Town and home.

"Hi, Clint! Welcome back!" Judi called when she saw Clint laying in the hammock on his deck at six thirty in the morning. He had come in late the night before and had cleaned up his computer messages and such, then crashed. He was still exhausted from so many days in buses and running around the country. No more of that for awhile!

He waved and called that he would come over in a while. She said she'd be right over. She had found a recipe for hojaldres with a bit of coconut and banana that was beyond delicious.

His computer dinged with an e-mail, so he went inside to read the message from Emanuel. *It seemed that the woman I was to contact died in a car accident the very night before I got here. At least this one wasn't after I contacted her! I spent two nights in Panamá City before going to San Blas. Veronica had sent, not just ten, but FIFTEEN thousand dollars! I already have a small medical and educational center being built. Things are wonderful. I actually have friends here! These people would work their asses (giggle) off to help.*

Wasn't it sad? The accident in San Diego, California? The church would sorely miss one such as Veronica and ... well, I supposed the project has ended permanently. All the directors were there when it happened.

Be in touch! - best wishes always to my best friend in the world! – Manu (as the people here call me)

Clint went to the world news site to check on what had happened in San Diego. Accident? The entire directorship of the project?

He found it.

Clint read the report, and sighed.

The computer dinged again. It was his private and personal e-mail service. Very few people knew about it, so it would be Manny, Dave, Sergio – not Judi. She was a hundred feet away.

It was from Raul Mali: *Hi, Clint. I'm in London and will return to Panamá in about two weeks to retire. I was not in California. I think I know who was.*

Emanuel is going to get a surprise. It seems there was an insurance policy recently taken out for various projects funded by a certain now-extinct group to be split up between their projects – which was The San Blas Mission Emanuel at the time. 5 mil. He can build a major hospital and school for the area. Some good will come from this.

Hope to see you soon. You are the one true friend I found in my business – at least, I hope you consider me as much of a friend as I consider you.

Clint sighed again. Right!

Well, what the hell? He was a great guy, in a lot of ways, and he hadn't prevaricated. He had arranged for Emanuel and the Indios to receive a true blessing. He had only eliminated a couple of growing cancers from the world. Maybe he was a friend!

Now. Fishing today?

No. Enough of that.

Judi came in the front door with a big plate of hojaldres. "Hi! I'm off to David today. Want to come along?"

Clint didn't hesitate for that one. "No."